Charlie, The Skunk Who Never Stunk

By

Jack Ellison

Copyright © 2024

By Jack Ellison

All rights reserved.

No part of this publication may be reproduced in any form, or by any means, electronic or mechanical, including photocopying, recording, or any information browsing, storage, or retrieval system, without permission in writing from Jack Ellison, Author.

A skunk sat on a stump. The stump said the skunk stunk, the skunk said the stump stunk. So who stunk, the stump or the skunk?

Well, it couldn't have been Charlie since his stinker couldn't stink. No matter how hard Charlie tried, he just could not make his stinker stink. All of the other skunks could stink really bad, but not Charlie. You see, Charlie was a unique skunk. Not only could he not stink but he was only 2" tall and 4" long, a really small skunk.

All of Charlie's friends were a lot bigger than Charlie and, therefore, left Charlie without someone who was equal to him.

There was one thing that Charlie had that none of the other skunks had, and that was intelligence! Charlie was one smart skunk. In school, he made straight A's and several of his skunk friends asked Charlie for help with their homework but Charlie never did their homework for them, instead he tutored them.

The bigger skunks became indebted to him because of this. Still, Charlie yearned for the ability to play football, basketball and other sports with his friends, but he could get seriously injured if he did participate in those sports because of his size.

Charlie had one very good friend...Willie. Willie was considerably overweight and lacking in athletic ability so at recess, he and Charlie would just sit and watch the others play.

The girl skunks also played their games at recess too. They played with dolls, jumped rope and played hop-scotch.

One day at recess, Charlie was leaning against a tree with a big book when all of a sudden, the ground began to vibrate, and the trees began to sway. What's going on, Charlie thought? It kept getting more intense, and then they heard a deafening growl...

GRRRRRAAAAARRRRREEEEEERLLL!

The skunks stopped playing, frozen with fear. All movement stopped, and then finally, after a few moments, everything returned to normal. Everybody went back to enjoying recess.

Then again it started only this time worse. The trees were being thrown to the ground and boulders were flying through the air then another horrible growl, only louder...
GRRRRRAAAAARRRRREEEEEERLLL!

Suddenly, out of the forest stepped the Biggest, the Baddest, the Ugliest, the Hairiest big bad Wolf anybody had ever seen. All of the skunks on that playground were frozen with fear; that is all except Charlie. He wasn't scared at all. For some reason, he was taking it all in.

The Wolf looked down upon all of the skunks and announced, "I am hungry and looking for a nice plump skunk for lunch." He looked around and focused in on Willie since he was just the size the Big Bad Wolf was looking for. "You are just the right one for my meal."

He lifted Willie up by his tail, opened his mouth wide showing grizzly, snarly teeth, and was about to drop Willie into his gullet when...

"Pardon me, Mr. Wolf, but I'm going to ask you to put my friend down." The Wolf looked around and said, "Who said that, I don't see anybody."
Charlie said, "I'm down here by your big toe."
"What are you, an ant?"
"No, Sir, I'm a Skunk; Charlie is my name."

"A Skunk eh? You're the tiniest skunk I've ever seen. Now, go away, boy, before I crush you with my big toe. You're bothering me."

"Mr. Wolf, I'm asking you nicely to put my best friend down. I will have to resort to other measures if you don't."

"Ha, ha, ha, ha." The wolf laughed, still holding Willie high in the air. What are you gonna do, spray me with a little perfume? I've got news for you Tiny, skunk spray doesn't bother me."
"This is your 3rd and final warning, Mr. Wolf. Put Willie down and leave or you will pay for it."

"Go ahead, Mini Mite...Give me your best. Ha, ha, ha." With that, Charlie turned around, raised his tail high into the air, and said, "Stinker, if you're ever gonna stink, please stink **NOW!!**"

12

Well, Charlie's stinker did the trick. He sprayed that wolf from the top of his head to the bottom of his big toe while releasing Willie unharmed.

Everybody agreed that Charlie's stink was the stinkest stink in the history of stunk. Even the skunks had to hold their noses.

Well, the Big Bad Wolf fell flat on his back then woke up and went running into the forest yipping, crying, and hollering for his Mommy while knocking over even more trees on the way out and he never came back to the School For Skunks ever again.

Needless to say, Charlie was the hero of the skunk playground. The skunks all threw Charlie up in the air praising him for his heroism. All of the boy skunks want Charlie on their team, and the girl skunks want Charlie for their boyfriend.

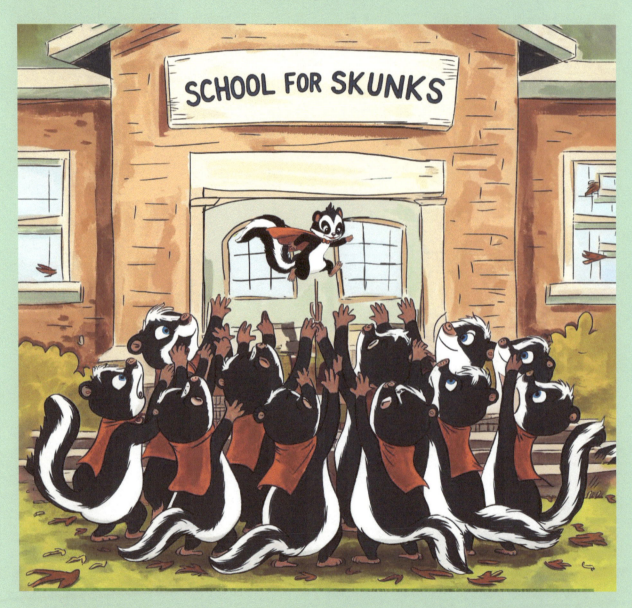

Now remember, Charlie was no longer the Skunk who Never Stunk. Now Charlie is the Skunk that really, really, really
STUUUNNNK!

Thank You

www.ingramcontent.com/pod-product-compliance
Ingram Content Group UK Ltd.
Pitfield, Milton Keynes, MK11 3LW, UK
UKHW051516150225

455113UK00003B/20